A Dream of Birds

By Shenaz Patel · Illustrated by Emmanuelle Tchoukriel

Translated by Edwige-Renée Dro

amazoncrossingkids

The bird you put inside a cage,

You will have to find it another name

For it is no longer a bird.

For my grandfather Doudou, who didn't close the door.

For Bertrand, with the heart of a cardinal bird.

For Lisa, with wings on her back . . .

—S. P.

For Salomé.

—E. T.

It is a beautiful summer morning.

In the blue sky, as blue as the color of a swimming pool, birds glide by
slowly, and the sun winks. With her bag on her back, Sara walks to school.
It is such a beautiful day that she'd rather go wander instead.
But the weekend is still far off, so she'll have to wait a bit more.

She comforts herself by dragging her feet.

She slows down even more when she passes by the last house
before the crossroad. It is a house that's a little crooked,
with old green shutters and a pointed roof that's slanted to the left.

But Sara is more intrigued by what's in the yard of the crooked house:
a tiny house with a red roof.

The day before, a truck came and dropped it off with the old man who lives there. And walking by, Sara wondered what use such a little house with no walls, only wire mesh, and topped with a bright red roof, could possibly have!

This morning she has the answer.

The old man has put birds inside the little house with the bright red roof. A lot of birds. A flock of parakeets of many different colors. Sara is in awe. She walks closer, and immediately the birds begin flapping around, drawing the colors of the rainbow. And making an impossible racket!

Chirping!

Trilling!

Suddenly, a big voice breaks out above the racket.

"What are you doing here, near my birdhouse?"

Sara turns around with a start.

The old man is standing just behind her, and he doesn't look like a kind person.
So she runs off. School awaits, and she's going to be late.

In class, Sara can't concentrate. Her mind keeps wandering.
She can't stop thinking about all those parakeets in the birdhouse
with the bright red roof.

She thinks about her grandfather.
She recalls being in the little yard outside his house.

When he was still around, and old, so old that he used to say that time
had forgotten him, she enjoyed going to see him in the afternoons.
Because in that little yard, every day, an incredible show took place.

At 3pm, the birds would begin to arrive, one by one, as if called
to a secret meeting. The cardinals, with their flaming feathers,
were the first to arrive and would take their places on the branches.
The Cape canaries, in their buttercup attire, would join them. And finally,
the lazy turtledoves with their smoky blue eyes, would arrive.

Dozens of birds would turn up—and ever so quickly, hundreds of them.
And it would be a concert of

peeping,

chirping,

cooing,

crooning,   singing,

larking,

And then, at exactly 4pm, Sara's grandfather would come out
of his house. Taking small, measured steps, he would walk toward
the center of his little yard, holding in his wrinkled and trembling hand
a tin mug filled with rice.

He would stand still for a moment, looking at the birds waiting for him.

Then, with a sweeping gesture as if opening a hand fan, he would throw
the grains of rice, and immediately the flock of impatient birds would
rush and pluck their food from the air.

Finally, in a great rustle of wings, they would depart, like a cloud
of colorful flowers carried off by the wind.

For the rest of the day, that's all Sara thinks about.
The birds flying from her grandfather's little yard. The parakeets
in the birdhouse with the bright red roof.

The next day, on her way to school, Sara stops in front of the
crooked house. She hesitates for a moment. Just for a moment.

Then she runs inside the yard. On seeing her, the parakeets begin
flapping around, drawing the colors of the rainbow—
and making a huge racket again!

Chirping!

Sara sees that the old man has not locked the door of the birdhouse.
She stretches out a hand. And she opens—wide—the door.

At first the birds don't move. As if they don't know what to do.

Then Sara enters the birdhouse, and she flaps her arms;
and just as suddenly, the parakeets take off.

All together, they fly out the open door, and in their flight, they make
a big rainbow that brightens the blue-swimming-pool sky.

Afterward,
afterward it is a storm.

The old man is furious. He hauls Sara home to her parents.
Her parents explain to her that what she did is wrong. That you can't
do that with other people's birds. That there are birds that are
not used to being free and may not know how to feed themselves.

Sara is punished.

That evening she goes to bed with a deep sadness in her heart.
She thinks about those birds who might not have anything to eat.

In the end she sleeps. And dreams . . .

Sara is on an island. An island called Cocos Island.
This island is like a birdhouse. A huge birdhouse with no wire mesh.
A gigantic, open-air birdhouse. And there are hundreds, thousands,
maybe tens of thousands of birds.

The brown noddies, also called makwaks on this island,

the lesser noddies,

the white terns,

the sooty terns.

All these birds there,
flying freely, sailing across the blue sky, carried by a ray of sunshine,
gliding in the air, singing their joy: Yeye, yeye, yeye, yeye!
And there are men and women there
who make sure that nobody bothers the birds.

In her sleep, Sara smiles. Somehow she knows that her birds
will be okay, that they will find their way.

And that she will too.

All will be well, so long as the world
has wings to dream.

Publisher's Note

This story takes place on Mauritius, an African island nation in the Indian Ocean,
where this book was first published. Cocos Island (Île aux Cocos),
the island in Sara's dream, is a real place too, situated off Rodrigues Island.
A tiny island close to Mauritius, Cocos Island is a nature preserve and
well-known for its colonies of seabirds.

Nearly four hundred species of birds live on the islands of the Indian Ocean,
and some of them can only be found here and nowhere else on our planet.
Sadly, many bird species in this area have gone extinct and will never be seen again.

While Sara's story is one of longing for freedom—for herself and for the birds in
the little red birdhouse—it's also a wish for our future: that we humans will learn
to take better care of our beautiful winged friends and keep dreaming of a better world.

Text by Shenaz Patel
Illustrations by Emmanuelle Tchoukriel
Text and illustrations copyright © 2020 by Atelier des Nomades
Translation copyright © 2022 by Edwige-Renée Dro

Previously published as *Reve D'Oiseau* and *A Dream of Birds* by Atelier des Nomades in Mauritius Island and France in 2020. Translated from French for Amazon Crossing Kids by Edwige-Renée Dro. First published in English by Amazon Crossing Kids in collaboration with Amazon Crossing in 2022.

Published by Amazon Crossing Kids, New York, in collaboration with Amazon Crossing
www.apub.com

Amazon, Amazon Crossing, and all related logos are trademarks of Amazon.com, Inc., or its affiliates.

ISBN-13: 9781662500930 (hardcover)
ISBN-10: 1662500939 (hardcover)

The illustrations were rendered in digital media.
Book design by Tanya Ross-Hughes

Printed in China
First Edition
10 9 8 7 6 5 4 3 2 1